DANGER GAMES

AVALANCHE!

Sue Graves

sundance™

 **sundance**™

Copyright © 2012 Sundance/Newbridge, LLC

Published by Sundance Publishing
33 Boston Post Road West, Suite 440, Marlborough, MA 01752
www.sundancepub.com

First published 2009 by
Rising Stars UK Ltd., 22 Grafton Street, London W1S 4EX

ISBN: 978-1-4207-3025-8

Printed by Nordica International Ltd.
Manufactured in Guangzhou, China
April, 2017
Nordica Job #: CA21700381
Sundance/Newbridge PO #: 228711

CHAPTER 1

It was a cold, wet Monday morning. Sima, Kojo, and Tom were having a coffee break in the office cafeteria. They worked at Dangerous Games, a computer games company.

Sima, Kojo, and Tom loved their jobs. Sima designed the computer games, and Kojo programmed them.

Tom had an amazing job. He tested the games and checked that they didn't have any bugs.

They got their coffees and sat down at an empty table.

"Did you have a good weekend?" Sima asked Tom, as she stirred sugar into her coffee.

"It was OK," said Tom, yawning. "But I've had better."

"I had nothing to do," said Kojo. "It was so boring. There wasn't even anything to watch on TV—just that stupid talent show again. It was *sooo* sad!"

"You two need a vacation!" said Sima. "That would cheer you up."

"No chance of that happening!" said Kojo. "The rent on my apartment is due. And my car broke down last week, too. I've got a massive repair bill. I can't afford a vacation."

Tom spotted a travel magazine lying on the next table. He picked it up and flipped through it. He stopped at a page about snowboarding vacations in the Alps.

"I'd love to go on a vacation like that," he said, tapping the page with his finger. "Imagine learning how to snowboard in the Alps. It would be awesome!"

"Me too," said Kojo. "But it's way too expensive."

"Yeah, you're right," said Tom. He threw the magazine back onto the table and picked up his coffee.

Sima looked thoughtful. She opened her bag and pulled out a notebook and pen. She started writing notes.

"We *might* be able to have a vacation," she said, after a few minutes.

"Do you have lots of money, Sima?" said Tom. "Did a rich uncle leave you a fortune in his will?"

"Or maybe you won the lottery?" said Kojo, laughing.

"No, I'm as broke as you two are," Sima replied. "But I've got an idea. Let's meet up at Frankie's Café at lunchtime, and I'll tell you all about it."

CHAPTER 2

It was still raining hard at lunchtime, and Frankie's Café was full. Sima and Tom got the sandwiches and the drinks. Kojo went to find a table near the window. Then Sima told them her plan.

"We all need a vacation," she said. "Right?"

"You've got that right!" said Kojo.

"But we can't afford one," continued Sima.

"Right again," said Tom.

"Then let's make a computer game about snowboarding," said Sima. "We could set it in the Alps just like the vacation in the travel magazine. Then we can test it for real like we've done before. We'll get a vacation in the Alps, and we can learn how to snowboard. Best of all, it won't cost us anything!"

"The woman's a genius," said Kojo.

"I know that," said Tom. "Sima's the best!" Sima looked embarrassed.

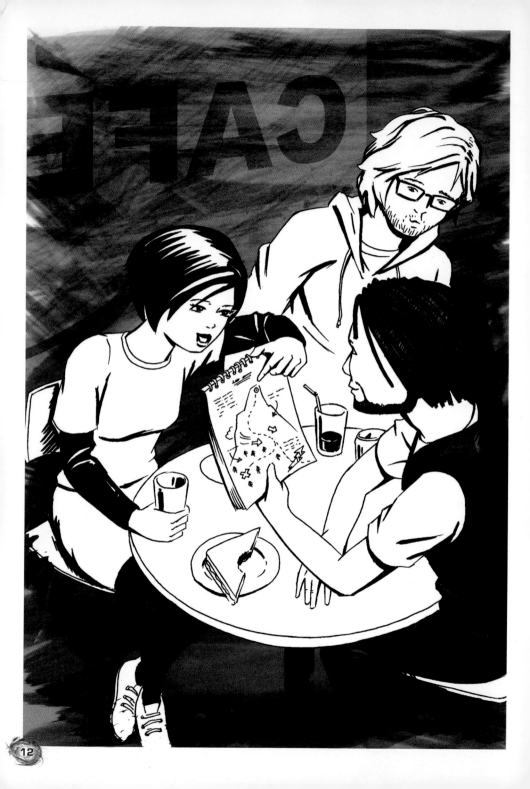

"So what happens in the game?" asked Kojo.

"You have to snowboard down a mountain," said Sima, "and there will be lots of obstacles in the way. You'll have to be really skillful to get around them. It'll be tricky."

She pulled her notebook out of her bag. "I made these notes this morning. It won't take me long to design the game. Can you program it, Kojo?"

"Sure," said Kojo. "If you give me the designs tomorrow, I'll get the programming done by Friday afternoon."

"You're on," said Sima. She bit into her sandwich and chewed thoughtfully. "This is going to be great."

That afternoon, Sima worked on the designs for the new game. She went on the Internet and found out about different styles of snowboarding. She also looked up information about the Alps to learn more about the mountains and the weather conditions.

Sima showed her designs to Kojo the next day.

"These are amazing, Sima!" he said. "I'll get started right away."

Kojo worked hard. By Friday afternoon, he had finished. The game was ready to be tested.

Sima, Tom, and Kojo waited for everyone to leave the office.

"It'll be cold in the Alps," said Sima. She put on her coat and long black boots.

Kojo put on his fleece and scarf. Tom zipped up his jacket and pulled his hat down low over his face.

"Ready?" asked Kojo.

"Ready," said Tom and Sima.

Kojo started up the game.

"Remember, we're playing this for real and anything could happen," he said. "It could be dangerous. Are you both still up for it?"

Sima and Tom nodded.

"OK," said Kojo. "We all have to touch the screen at the same time. Don't forget, the game is only over when we hear the words *Game over.*"

They all put their hands on the screen. A bright light flashed, and they shut their eyes tightly.

CHAPTER 3

The bright light faded. Kojo, Tom, and Sima felt snow falling on their faces. They opened their eyes and looked around. They were standing on the side of a huge mountain, and it was freezing cold. Far below, they could see a small village. There were ramps and other obstacles on the mountain.

Down one side of the mountain was a thick line of pine trees. Three snowboards were propped up near the trees.

LOOK OVER THERE.

They walked through the snow toward the trees.
Tom grabbed a snowboard and jumped onto it,
but the board shot out from under him.
He landed with a thud in the snow.

WIPEOUT!

YOU TRY IT IF YOU'RE SO SMART.

54:00

Sima stepped carefully onto her board and strapped her boots into the bindings. She held out her arms to keep her balance as the board moved forward.

"Wow, I love this," she said. "Come on, you two. It's easy!"

Kojo and Tom got on their boards. After a few minutes, they had the hang of it, too.

"Let's try out the obstacle course," said Kojo. "It looks really cool!"

"OK, you go first," said Sima.

But just then, Tom spotted something moving in the trees.

CHAPTER 4

Out of the trees came a snowmobile.
A man in a mask was riding it. Within
seconds he was alongside Kojo, Tom, and
Sima. He was holding a snow cannon.

"Let's make the game more interesting,"
the man said nastily. He raised the cannon
and aimed it at Kojo. Tom pushed Kojo out
of the way. Kojo fell onto the snow.

The man turned toward Tom
and glared at him.

Tom jumped off his snowboard and threw it at the man. Then he started to run for the trees. The snowmobile followed. The man blasted the snow cannon at Tom. A powerful jet of snow narrowly missed him.

The snowmobile was gaining on Tom.

WE'VE GOT TO DO SOMETHING!

Tom desperately doubled back. The snowmobile swung around, getting closer and closer.

Quickly, Sima hurled her snowboard into the path of the snowmobile. The driver lost control. He jumped out just before the vehicle hit a rock. There was a loud explosion as the snowmobile burst into flames.

The man ran off into the trees.

"Phew!" gasped Tom.
"That was a close call. What's going on? Who was that man?"

"I don't know," Sima replied. "I didn't design the game to turn out like this."

Kojo looked worried. "I think some sort of virus has gotten into the computer program," he said.

"What's going to happen?" said Tom.

"I have no idea," said Kojo.
"A virus can cause all sorts of problems. Let's get down the mountain as fast as we can."

They lined up their snowboards, but before they could get on them they heard a low rumbling sound.

LOOK!

WHAT'S THAT?

Tom pointed to the top of the mountain. The mountain itself seemed to be moving. Snow and rocks were sliding down toward them.

THE EXPLOSION HAS TRIGGERED AN AVALANCHE! IF WE DON'T GET OUT OF HERE, WE'LL BE KILLED.

Sima, Tom, and Kojo jumped onto their snowboards. They slid as fast as they could around the obstacles to get down the mountain, but the avalanche was gaining speed. Snow, rocks, and uprooted trees tumbled down after them. A large rock spun into Tom and knocked him over. He landed in the snow.

Kojo and Sima turned and looked back. There was a loud creaking sound. They looked up and saw a wall of snow heading for Tom. But before they could warn him, the wall of snow crashed into him and buried him completely.

CHAPTER 5

The avalanche lasted for several minutes. Kojo and Sima curled up into tight balls and covered their heads with their arms. Then, as quickly as it had started, the avalanche stopped. A strange silence fell over the mountain. Sima crawled over to Kojo.

Kojo wiped the snow from his face. "Tom's buried under the snow," he said urgently. "We've got to get him out. There's no time to lose."

Sima pointed to some branches lying in the snow.

"Let's use these as probes," she said. "If we push them into the snow, we may be able to find Tom."

Sima and Kojo struggled up the mountainside to where they had last seen Tom. They pushed the probes into the snow again and again.

"Can you feel anything yet?" asked Kojo.

Sima shook her head sadly.

A moment later, Kojo let out a yell.

"There's something under here," he said.
"It must be Tom. Help me dig him out."

Sima ran over to Kojo. They clawed at
the snow with their hands. Suddenly
they saw Tom's arm.

They dug frantically. Soon they were
able to pull Tom out. They brushed
the snow away from Tom's face.
His lips were blue, and there was
no sign of life.

Kojo and Sima turned Tom
onto his back.

Sima rubbed his hands.
They were ice cold.

Kojo tried to keep calm. He felt
Tom's wrist.

"I can feel a weak pulse," he said.
"He's still with us, just barely."

He breathed air into Tom's mouth,
again and again.

Suddenly Tom sputtered. He took a deep gasp of air and opened his eyes. Slowly the color returned to his face.

"What happened?" he asked.

"The avalanche buried you," said Sima. She was crying with relief. "I thought you were dead, but Kojo saved you."

Tom sat up. He brushed the snow off his hair and jacket. Then he grinned at Sima.

The next moment, a bright light lit up the mountain. Tom, Sima, and Kojo shut their eyes tightly.

A loud voice said, "Game over!"

Then the light faded, and they opened their eyes. They were back in the office. Kojo's computer screen was flashing with the words *Game over.*

"That was a fantastic game," said Kojo.

Sima looked serious. "It wasn't," she said. "Tom could have died. The virus made the game too dangerous. We should have programmed a virus checker into the game."

Kojo looked upset. "That was my fault," he said. "I should have done that. I'm really sorry."

Tom gave Sima a hug. He grinned at Kojo. "Stop worrying about it, you two. There's no harm done. And we can turn our adventure into an amazing computer game."

"But we won't test it for real again," said Kojo.

"No way!" said Tom. "I'm staying firmly outside the computer next time. But right now, let's go out for dinner and celebrate our new game. While we're eating, we can think of a name for it."

"There's only one *possible* name," said Sima.

"What's that?" asked Kojo.

"Avalanche!" said Sima. "Duh!" And she rolled her eyes.

Kojo and Tom laughed.

GLOSSARY OF TERMS

Alps a mountain range in Europe

avalanche a fall of snow, ice, and rocks down a mountain

bugs mistakes in a computer program

obstacle a barrier that is put in your way to make getting from one place to another more difficult

probes tools used to search for something by poking around

program to write instructions for a computer to tell it what to do

snow cannon a machine which makes snow and blasts it out

snowmobile a vehicle designed to travel across snow

virus a computer program that damages or destroys information stored in a computer

THINK ABOUT IT

1. What keeps Sima, Kojo, and Tom from taking a vacation?

2. What plan does Sima come up with so that they can all have a vacation?

3. Why does Sima go on the Internet before designing the snowboarding game?

4. Kojo says that the explosion triggered the avalanche. How could you explain his thinking?

5. Is snowboarding a sport you would like to try? Why or why not?

ABOUT THE AUTHOR

Sue Graves has taught school for thirty years. She has been writing for more than ten years and has written well over a hundred books for children and young adults.

"Nearly everyone loves computer games. They are popular with all age groups—especially young adults. But I've often thought it would be amazing to play a computer game for real. To be in on the action would be the best experience ever! That's why I wrote these stories. I hope you enjoy reading them as much as I've enjoyed writing them for you."

READ STREET WARS FIRST TO FIND OUT
HOW THE ADVENTURE BEGINS!

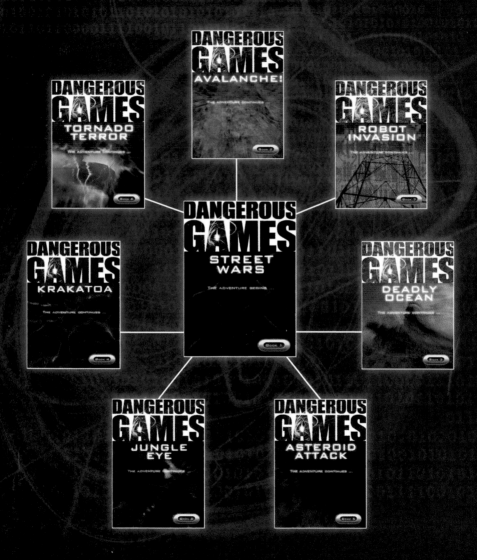